Secret Kingdom

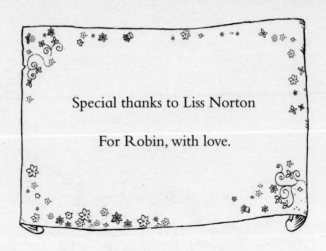

Special thanks to Liss Norton

For Robin, with love.

ORCHARD BOOKS

First published in Great Britain in 2014 by Orchard Books
This edition published in 2017 by The Watts Publishing Group

1 3 5 7 9 10 8 6 4 2

© 2014 Hothouse Fiction Limited
Illustrations © Orchard Books 2014

A CIP catalogue record for this book is available from the British Library.

ISBN 978 1 40835 294 6

Printed in Great Britain by Clays Ltd, St Ives plc

The paper and board used in this book are made from wood from responsible sources

Orchard Books
An imprint of Hachette Children's Group
Part of The Watts Publishing Group Limited
Carmelite House, 50 Victoria Embankment, London EC4Y 0DZ

An Hachette UK Company
www.hachette.co.uk
www.hachettechildrens.co.uk

Series created by Hothouse Fiction
www.hothousefiction.com

Glitter Bird

ROSIE BANKS

ORCHARD

This is the Secret Kingdom

Leafy Lands

Contents

A Message From Trixi

"Ready?" asked Jasmine Smith.

"You bet!" chorused her best friends Ellie Macdonald and Summer Hammond. It was half term and the three girls were in Summer's bedroom. Jasmine had brought a DVD, *Animal Acrobats*, for them to watch because it was too rainy to play outside.

"Here goes then," Jasmine said, flicking back her long dark hair. She pressed play on the DVD player and sat down on Summer's bed. "I love this film, it's really funny. Especially the bit where the baby owls are learning to fly."

Summer smiled dreamily and stroked her cute little black cat, Rosa, who was lying beside her on the bed.

"I love it when we get to fly in the Secret Kingdom. It's such fun!"

Ellie wrinkled her nose. "I don't," she said. "I prefer staying on the ground, thanks! But I *do* love going to the Secret Kingdom." She smiled, feeling a thrill of excitement as she thought about the amazing secret they all shared.

The girls looked after a magic box that could whisk them off to a wonderful, enchanted land filled with mermaids, unicorns and other amazing creatures. Summer, Jasmine and Ellie were Very Important Friends of the magical kingdom, and went there every time kind King Merry needed help to keep the land safe from his mean sister, Queen Malice.

Ellie kneeled down by the bed and tickled Rosa. Purring, the little cat rolled over and batted her fingers playfully. The movement set two gold charms on

her collar jingling. One was
shaped like a flower
and the other
like a crown.

"I wish
we could
go back to
the Secret
Kingdom
right now,"
said Ellie,
touching the

charms gently. "We need to return these
charms to the last two Animal Keepers."

A few days ago, King Merry had
summoned the four Animal Keepers from
their shield with ancient magic. These
magical creatures – a puppy, a seal, a
bird and a lion cub – came out of the

shield every hundred years and travelled through the Secret Kingdom for one week, spreading fun, kindness, friendship and bravery all around the land. But mean Queen Malice had cast a horrible spell, meaning that they now brought the opposite wherever they went – misery, meanness, squabbling and cowardice!

"I'm sure Trixi will send us a message soon," Summer said. Their friend Trixibelle was a Royal Pixie. She worked for King Merry and used the Magic Box to get in touch with the girls whenever help was needed in the Secret Kingdom.

The girls had spent lots of their half term holiday at Summer's house because they needed to take Rosa with them when they went to the Secret Kingdom.

In their first adventure with the Puppy Keeper, Summer, Ellie and Jasmine had attached the four Animal Keepers' charms onto Rosa's collar to keep them safe. Once the charms were returned to each Animal Keeper, Queen Malice's spell would be broken!

Ellie gave Rosa one last stroke then sat back on the bed.

On the TV, the film was starting. Three owlets were trying to pluck up the courage to jump off a branch and fly for the first time. One of them ran along the branch with his wings spread wide, then chickened out at the last moment and stopped dead. His sister, who was running along behind, bumped into his back.

The girls giggled.

"That first owl looks so grumpy!" Summer said, laughing.

"And look at his sister!" said Jasmine as the second owl flapped her wings crossly.

Suddenly Ellie sprang off the bed. "Oh, wow!" she gasped, pointing at Summer's desk.

"What?" asked Summer, looking round.

"The Magic Box!" gasped Ellie. "It's glowing!" She lifted the box off the desk, her heart pounding with excitement.

The wooden box was beautifully
carved with pictures of mermaids,
unicorns and other wonderful creatures.
An oval mirror, surrounded by six
glittering green gems, was set into its lid.

Ellie put the box on the bed and
they all peered into the mirror, waiting
breathlessly for Trixi's message to appear.
The mirror began to glow and magical
words appeared. Jasmine read them out:

"The Keeper you seek is passing by
The place where pixies learn to fly.
You must break the queen's mean spell
To make friendships strong and well!"

"The third Animal Keeper!" breathed
Summer.

"And the riddle mentions friendships,

so it must be the Bird Keeper we need to find this time," Ellie added. "She looks after friendship."

"A place where pixies learn to fly…" Jasmine frowned thoughtfully. "Any ideas?"

Before the others could reply, the box flew open. Inside were six compartments holding magical treasures. There was an icy hourglass that could freeze time, a tiny unicorn horn that let them talk to animals, a pearl to make them invisible, a glittering crystal that could control the weather and a tiny bag of glitter dust – just enough for them to make one wish. The sixth compartment contained a map of the Secret Kingdom. As they watched, it floated up into the air and Summer caught it. She spread it out on the bed.

The girls leaned over to see it better, and Rosa pushed in between Summer and Jasmine so she could look too.

At first glance, the map looked fairly ordinary, showing the crescent moon shape of the kingdom. But when they peered closer they could see unicorns cantering across a meadow and gnomes climbing tall ladders in Wildflower Wood. Even the golden flags on King Merry's Enchanted Palace were fluttering in the breeze. It was so magical!

"Remember when we visited Trixi's aunt?" said Summer. "Wasn't the Pixie Flying School nearby?"

"You're right!" Ellie agreed excitedly. "Let's see if we can spot Aunt Maybelle's cottage."

"Ooh, look at the shield!" said Jasmine. There was a shield at the top of the map that was divided into four quarters. The two lowest quarters showed a puppy and a seal – the two Animal Keepers that the girls had already helped. The two top quarters were empty, waiting for the return of the Bird Keeper and the brave lion cub. And one of them was shimmering with green light!

Screwing up her eyes to help her see better, Ellie bent low over the map and stared at the shield. "I think that shimmering picture is a forest," she said.

"So we need to find a forest on the map." Summer scanned it quickly. "There!" she said. "There are lots of trees in the Leafy Lands. That must be where we're going!"

Excitedly, the girls placed their hands over the green gems on the Magic Box's lid. "Leafy Lands!" they cried.

There was a brilliant flash and the room was suddenly filled with silver sparkles. Then a tiny pixie appeared, flying on her leaf. She was wearing a blue dress with a cute flower-petal skirt and a tiny bluebell hat was sitting on top of her tangle of blonde hair.

"Trixi!" the girls cried, overjoyed to see her. They knew that in just a few moments, they'd be enjoying another wonderful Secret Kingdom adventure!

Flying High!

"Hello, girls," Trixi said with a sad smile.

"What's wrong, Trixi?" Ellie asked.

"Today's the day of the Leaping Leaf Competition," the little pixie said, sitting down on her leaf. "Young pixies from the Pixie Flying School pair up to demonstrate how well they can fly, but there's a problem with this year's contest."

"What sort of problem?" asked Jasmine anxiously. She was pretty sure that whatever it was, Queen Malice would be behind it!

"It's best if I show you," Trixi said. "Let's go to the Secret Kingdom!"

The girls leaped up, eager to be off on another adventure. Rosa sprang into Summer's arms.

Trixi tapped her pixie ring and chanted:

"Pixie magic, lift us high,
And take us where the pixies fly!"

A glittery whirlwind came whooshing out of her ring. It began to spin around the girls, twirling faster and faster until they were lifted off their feet.

"Here we go!" cried Ellie excitedly.

A moment later, they landed with a gentle bump and saw that they were in a beautiful forest full of the most enormous trees they'd ever seen. They seemed to stretch up and up for miles.

"What huge flowers!" exclaimed Ellie. Yellow flowers as big as dinner plates grew on every side. Their sweet perfume filled the air.

"And look at our clothes," said
Jasmine, twirling around in delight.
They were wearing dresses in the same
style as Trixi's, with sleeveless tops and
flower-petal skirts. Jasmine's was pink,
Ellie's was purple and Summer's was
yellow. They wore matching shoes,
too, and their tiaras
had magically
appeared on
their heads.
The glittery
tiaras showed
that they
were Very
Important
Friends of King
Merry and the
Secret Kingdom!

"These dresses are lovely, Trixi. Thank you," said Summer. Then she noticed that Trixi wasn't there. "Trixi?" she called, looking round in surprise. "Where are you?"

"Here I am!" Trixi called back. She came zooming out from behind a tree on her leaf.

They all stared. "Wow, Trixi, you're huge!" Jasmine cried.

The girls giggled and ducked as their pixie friend swooped over their heads on her giant leaf!

"Trixi's not huge," Ellie realised with a laugh.

"We're small! That's why everything looks so big."

"That's right," said Trixi with a mischievous grin. "I've made you pixie-size, just for a little while. It will make travelling around here so much easier! I've got some practise leaves for you, too. All the leaves we pixies use come from the Heart Tree, which is right at the centre of the Leafy Lands. The leaves will help you fly just like real pixies!"

"Fantastic!" cried Jasmine. "I love flying! Ooh, I bet this will be even more fun than the time we flew into the kingdom on King Merry's royal swans! Or when we flew on Santa's sleigh!"

But as Jasmine jumped up and down with excitement, Ellie turned pale.

"I'm not sure I want to fly," she said

nervously, tucking a red curl behind one ear. "I really don't like heights!"

Summer took her hand. "It'll be okay. We'll stick together." She called to Rosa, who had also been shrunk to pixie-cat size, and they all ran forward, ducking under the tall flowers.

Trixi led them into a clearing. "Here we are," she said, gesturing to three leaves lying on the ground. They were large and broad with curled-up sides, almost like low walls. One of them had an acorn cup attached to the stalk.

"They look pretty safe," Ellie said, relieved. "Thanks, Trixi."

"I bet mine is that one," Summer said, pointing to the leaf with the acorn. "The acorn cup makes a cute little place for Rosa to sit!"

"Exactly right!" agreed Trixi with a smile.

Jasmine couldn't wait. She climbed up eagerly onto the nearest leaf and stood up confidently "How do I make it go?" she grinned.

"Lean forward," Trixi said. "Like this."

She leaned forward on her own leaf and it flew across the clearing.

Holding her arms out to help her balance, Jasmine copied Trixi's movement. The leaf rose smoothly into the air. "Wow, I'm flying!" she cheered. "Fantastic!"

"Don't go too fast!" Trixi warned. "You don't know how to steer yet."

Jasmine moved her foot a little to the left and the leaf turned. "I think I do!" she called excitedly.

"Come on, Rosa," Summer said. She kneeled on her leaf and Rosa jumped into the acorn cup. She sat down with her ears pricked up eagerly. "Here goes, then." Summer pushed back her blonde pigtails, then leaned forward cautiously. The leaf took off, wobbling a little.

"You're doing fine, Summer," called Trixi as the leaf steadied itself.

Summer beamed at her. "It's so fun. No wonder you love whizzing around on your leaf so much!"

Ellie watched her friends flying. *I can do this*, she told herself as she climbed into her leaf and sat down. Gripping the curled sides tightly, she leaned forward a tiny bit. The leaf rose half a metre off the ground, then flew forwards.

"If you want to go faster, lean forward more," Trixi called. "To slow down or stop, lean back. And leaning to the left or right makes it turn that way."

Jasmine leaned forward and her leaf zoomed away into the trees. "This is amazing!" she yelled, steering in and out between the enormous trunks.

"Come on, Rosa," said Summer. "Let's catch up!" She sped after Jasmine.

Trixi flew along beside Ellie.

"Are we far from the Pixie Flying School?" Ellie asked.

"No, we'll be there in a few minutes. We're quite close to Rose Cottage, where Aunt Maybelle lives."

Trixi flew ahead and Ellie sped up a little so she wouldn't be left behind. She was starting to enjoy herself, though she was happy not to fly as high as Summer and Jasmine!

"Look!" cried Summer. She zoomed down to the ground.

They all flew over to see what she'd found. A long line of cute creatures was wriggling up one of the trees. They were pink and fluffy with friendly faces.

"What are they, Trixi?" asked Ellie.

"Glow-worms," Trixi replied.

The girls stroked them and the glow-worms made a happy humming sound. Their tails lit up in a rainbow display of colours.

"They're so sweet," Summer said.

"They are," agreed Trixi. "And they're helpful, too. They light the woodland paths around the Leafy Lands at night so everyone can find their way around."

"I wish I had one as a pet," Summer said. "I'd be able to read in bed without having to get up to switch on the light!"

The girls said goodbye to the glow-worms, then flew on. They soon spotted the Pixie Flying School ahead. They'd flown over the school once before, when they'd visited Aunt Maybelle, but it looked much more impressive close up!

It was built in a square around a large lawn and had glittering white walls and a golden roof that shone in the sunshine. In each corner stood a tall tower, topped with a purple flag. Lots of identical leaves were lying on the grass and a few pixies were sitting beside them. They all looked grumpy.

As they flew closer to the school, the girls heard a cross voice above their heads: "Let me steer! You're doing it all wrong."

"No, I'm not!" yelled another voice. "You don't know what you're doing!"

Looking up, they saw a leaf plummeting towards the ground. The two young pixies on board were too busy arguing to notice what was happening.

"You're useless at flying!" bawled one.

"You're just jealous because I'm better at it than you are," snapped the other.

In just a few seconds the leaf would smash straight into the ground!

"You're going to crash!" cried Summer.

Golden Glitter

The girls steered their leaves towards the squabbling pixies as they hurtled towards the ground.

Trixi hurriedly tapped her ring and chanted:

"Pixie magic, hear my call,
And save these squabblers from
their fall!"

The leaf jerked to a stop only a few centimetres from the ground. "That was your fault!" the pixies yelled at one another. They jumped off the leaf and stomped away in a huff with their leaf floating behind them.

"They didn't even say thank you," said Summer, staring after them in astonishment.

Trixi sighed. "We'd better talk to Madame Aviala, the headmistress, and find out exactly what's going on."

"Tell us about the flying competition, Trixi," said Ellie as they flew closer to the school.

"Well, it's a really important contest," Trixi said. "The competitors are in their final year of school so they're all very good fliers. They work in pairs, performing all sorts of daring dives and soaring swoops. King Merry is the judge and the winning pair are crowned the best fliers in the kingdom! After they've won they are given their grown-up leaves and they travel all around the land, using special pixie magic to teach other flying creatures all kinds of brilliant tricks and skills."

"The competition sounds great fun," said Jasmine.

"It is – *usually* – but this year something's gone wrong," sighed Trixi. "The pixies are all squabbling. They won't work together as a team, and the competition is *all* about teamwork! Goodness knows how it will be able to go ahead, but we can't cancel it. The winners help King Merry's royal swans, and the bubblebees and all sorts of other flying creatures. Without the help of these pixies, the magical creatures of the Secret Kingdom wouldn't be able to swoop or dive or glide properly."

The friends flew down into the courtyard and landed just as Madame Aviala came out of the school. She was an elegant pixie dressed all in purple and wearing a hat made from a pansy. "Trixi, thank goodness you're here!" she cried.

"My friends have come to help," said Trixi. "This is Jasmine, Ellie and Summer."

"The human girls from the Other Realm!" Madame Aviala shook hands with them eagerly. "I've heard all about you. If anyone can put things right, it will be you three."

"We'll do our best," said Jasmine. "Why don't you tell us what's been going on?"

Madame Aviala sighed. "Everything was fine until this morning. The pixies were practising for the competition when a beautiful bird flew over."

"That must have been the Bird Keeper," said Summer, remembering the stunning blue-and-lilac bird they'd met at King Merry's palace a few days earlier.

"I was inside, working on the costumes for the show," Madame Aviala continued. "The bird flew round and round, singing a beautiful song and showering the pixies with golden glitter." She pointed up into the sky. "You can still see the glitter in the air."

"When did the pixies start arguing, Madame Aviala?" asked Ellie.

"Just after the bird flew away. Until then everyone had been fine."

Jasmine frowned thoughtfully. "The Bird Keeper usually spreads friendship wherever she goes, but this time—"

"The arguments started as soon as she flew away," Summer finished for her. "So Queen Malice's spell must make her take away all the friendship when she flies over."

"Yes!" said Ellie excitedly. "And because the glitter comes from the bird, if the glitter touches you it makes you unfriendly, too!"

The girls watched a group of pixies walking past. They were all shouting at the tops of their voices. "We are *not* doing a triple back flip," one of them yelled crossly.

"I'm not going to be
your partner then!"
snapped another.

"Trixi,"
asked Jasmine
curiously as
Madame Aviala
ran over to try
to soothe the
squabbling pixies.
"Why does your
flying leaf look different to

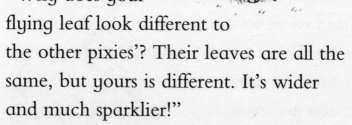

the other pixies'? Their leaves are all the
same, but yours is different. It's wider
and much sparklier!"

Trixi smiled and stroked her precious
leaf. "All pixies have the same leaves
until they finish learning to fly. Only
then are they given a leaf to suit their

strength and skills in a special graduation ceremony."

Just as the girls were about to ask more about the ceremony, Madame Aviala came back. With a gasp, Summer saw that the older pixie had tears in her eyes. She rushed to hug her.

"We've been working towards this competition for months," Madame Aviala said sadly. "And now all that hard work will be wasted!"

Trixi used her magic to create a handkerchief and the kindly teacher blew her nose. "And who

will help all the other flying creatures
to perfect their skills? Imagine if King
Merry's royal swans didn't know how to
fly in formation..." She dabbed at her
eyes. "Please say you'll help."

"We will!" promised Summer. "We just
need to work out a plan."

"We should head off straightaway and
search for the Bird Keeper," Jasmine said.
She noticed a sparkle on her shoulder
and quickly brushed it away.

"No, that won't work," said Summer.
"We need to look for clues first,
otherwise we could end up flying all over
the place and not spotting her at all. I
think we should try to make the words
appear on the charm, like we did for the
Puppy Keeper and the Seal Keeper."

"Let's talk to the pixies," Ellie

suggested. "One of them might have seen what direction the bird went when she flew away."

"No, Ellie, we have to look for clues," said Summer crossly.

"We *must* start searching for the bird!" snapped Jasmine, stamping her foot.

"Well, *I'm* asking the pixies," Ellie shouted. She marched across the courtyard, but Summer and Jasmine zoomed after her on their leaves.

"We *all* need to search for the bird," Jasmine insisted, blocking her path.

"First we need to find some clues!" yelled Summer. She glared at Ellie and Jasmine. Why couldn't they see that she was right?

Trixi came whizzing over. "What's going on?" she asked, sounding shocked.

"*They* don't know what they're talking about," said Jasmine. She soared up into the sky on her leaf. "I'll find the Bird Keeper on my own!"

"*I'll* find her by looking for clues that show where she's been!" Summer shouted after her. She made sure that Rosa was sitting down safely in her acorn cup, then flew off towards the woods.

"The pixies will tell me where to look," Ellie called. "And *I'll* find the Bird Keeper before either of you. So there!"

Falling Out

Jasmine sped into the forest, looking
all around for the Bird Keeper. She felt
cross and grumpy. *Why can't Ellie and
Summer see that my idea is best?*

After flying for a little while, she
spotted a boy and girl pixie sitting on
a tree branch. They had their backs to
each other and looked very cross.

"Hello, have you seen a pretty
multicoloured bird?" she asked, flying
down to them.

"Yes, it flew over the school earlier," said the boy pixie.

"*I* didn't see a multicoloured bird," said the girl pixie with a sneer. "*You're* telling a fib!"

"I'm not telling a fib!" shouted the boy. "You didn't see the bird because you were too busy chatting to your friends when we *should* have been practising for the competition!"

The pixies stuck their tongues out at each other and moved even further apart.

Jasmine hopped off her leaf and sat down on the branch next to the pixies. "I'm Jasmine," she said. "What seems to be the problem?"

"I'm Holly and this is Tiggs," said the girl pixie. "We *used* to be best friends, but we've had a fight. And now we can't do our midair leaf swap in the flying competition."

"Why not?" Jasmine asked.

"Because I don't trust *her* any more," said Tiggs, jumping to his feet and pointing angrily at Holly. "I heard her say to one of her friends that she was bored of practising with me! And we've been working so hard. Our leaves have to be exactly level to perform the midair swap. But if Holly doesn't care about the competition she might not care if her leaf's in the wrong place, and I could fall to the ground!"

"You've been really grumpy with me today too!" retorted Holly. "How do I know I can trust *you*?"

"I know just how you feel," Jasmine said. She was going to tell the pixies how cross she was with Summer and Ellie for not coming with her to look for the Bird Keeper, then she suddenly realised that she really missed them. "I've fallen out with my best friends too," she said sadly. "But you can still work together to practise your flying trick."

Holly and Tiggs shook their heads.

"I'm not practising with her until she says sorry!" said Tiggs stubbornly.

"And I'm not saying sorry until *he* apologises for being so grumpy!" cried

Holly, glaring at Tiggs.

"Look, why don't we forget about saying sorry for now," said Jasmine, putting an arm around Tiggs and Holly. "The competition starts soon and it's really important that you try to work together. You've worked so hard. Let's try the move again. I'll fly underneath you while you practise," she promised. "Just in case one of you falls."

"I suppose we could give it a try," said Tiggs doubtfully. The two pixies stood up on their leaves.

"Go on then," said Jasmine. "You'll be brilliant!"

The two pixies raced off at top speed, side by side.

Jasmine flew just below them. She wished Ellie and Summer were here too!

"Now!" shouted Tiggs.

Jasmine leaned forward as far as she could without falling over and steered her leaf directly under the narrow gap between Holly and Tiggs's leaves.

The two pixies leaped across the gap, then jumped back again. Then they slowed right down.

"What do you think?" Tiggs asked, looking down at Jasmine.

"Great!" said Jasmine. "But I know how you can make it even better. Try bending your knees and throwing your arms up when you land, and hold that pose for a few seconds. Like this." She showed them what she meant. "Ta-daaaa!"

"I like that idea," Holly said eagerly. She looked anxiously at Tiggs. "What do you think?"

He nodded.

"Good," said Jasmine. "And how about turning in midair as you jump, so you land facing each other."

The pixies tried out her suggestions.

"That feels good," said Tiggs, beaming at Jasmine and then at Holly.

"That's settled then," said Jasmine, pleased. "I can't wait to see you fly in the competition this afternoon!"

Ellie ran into the school, hoping to find some pixies to talk to. She was sure one of them must have seen which way the Bird Keeper was heading.

Suddenly a door opened and Madame Aviala hurried through, carrying an enormous box. It was so big that she could hardly see over it!

"Look out!" cried Ellie. She tried to jump out of the way but it was too late. Madame Aviala bumped into her and the box toppled over, spilling its contents.

"Wow!" Ellie exclaimed as she crouched down to pick things up. "This stuff is amazing!" There were lengths of sparkly cloth, sequins, coils of glittering wire, and fake fur and feathers in every colour of the rainbow. "What's all this for?"

"We always make special flying costumes together on the morning of the contest," replied the headmistress. "But the pixies who were meant to help have gone off in a huff so I'll have to do it all myself."

"I'll help," offered Ellie. She was still feeling a bit grumpy, but thinking of all different ways to use that glittery wire and those gorgeous pieces of fabric was making her feel much better! *What a shame Summer and Jasmine aren't here*, she thought. The pink sparkly fabric made her think of Jasmine, and she knew Summer would love the furry leopard-print cloth!

Madame Aviala brightened up. "Really? That would be wonderful, Ellie."

They piled everything back into the box, then carried it into an empty classroom where plain leotards and leggings hung on a rail. "These are the clothes the pixies will be wearing in the competition," said Madame Aviala.

"And we need to turn them into something special."

"No problem." Ellie lifted down a purple leotard. "I'm going to make this one a butterfly costume with some wire and sequins." As she started to coil the wire into wing shapes  she began to hum, feeling much happier!

Summer and Rosa flew into the woods. "Look out for the Bird Keeper, Rosa," said Summer, leaning over to tickle her

under the chin. The little
cat gave a happy purr
as if she understood
just what Summer
was saying!

They flew low,
weaving in and
out between the
massive tree
trunks. Summer
kept her eyes open
for sparkles that
would show where the bird had been.

Suddenly Summer heard somebody
crying. She slowed down and looked
around. "Hello," she called. "What's
wrong? Can I help?"

"Nobody can help," replied a quavery
voice.

Summer flew down
towards the voice
and found a
little pixie boy
sitting behind
a bush. His
eyes were red
and puffy from
crying and he was
wringing out a very
wet handkerchief.

"Are you okay?" she asked, hovering
beside him.

Rosa jumped down from the leaf
and nudged the little pixie with her
head. Then she settled down on his lap,
purring.

"Rosa likes you!" Summer said with a
smile.

The pixie stroked Rosa's soft fur. "My name's Pip," he said.

"What's wrong?" asked Summer.

"Each year Madame Aviala chooses one younger pixie to perform in the grand finale of the competition," Pip sniffed. "This year I was chosen and I was really looking forward to it. But now everyone is being so mean that I don't want to do it any more!" He began to sob again.

Rosa reached up and touched his nose with hers, then rubbed her soft head on his wet cheek.

"Rosa thinks you can do it," said Summer. "And so do I!" She wished Ellie and Jasmine were there. They'd know exactly what to say to make poor Pip feel better.

"Why do you think Madame Aviala picked you over all the other young pixies to star in the grand finale?" Summer asked Pip.

The little pixie shrugged sadly.

"It's because she knows how good you are." Summer squeezed Pip's hand. "You can't let her down. She's depending on you."

"I suppose so," sniffed Pip, looking a bit more cheery.

"Why don't you go back to school and practise," said Summer cheerily. "I'm sure you'll feel much better when you're back on your leaf!"

Pip gave Rosa a hug, then stood up. "You're right," he said, blowing his nose. "That's what I'll do. I'm going back to the flying school!" And with that, the little pixie jumped onto his leaf.

"Good luck!" Summer called after him as he zipped away between the trees.

Suddenly she noticed that the flower charm on Rosa's collar was glowing. She peered closely at the charm. The first two lines of the spell had appeared! Summer read them out loud:

"To bring me back, speak loud and clear,
No matter if I'm far or near..."

Summer gave Rosa a hug. "Helping

Pip has made the words appear!" she said happily. "Let's find Ellie and Jasmine and show them the riddle."

Summer jumped on her leaf, making sure Rosa was safely sitting in her acorn seat. As she raced through the trees, she hoped she'd meet up with Jasmine and Summer soon. They might have fallen out, but they were her best friends and the three of them *had* to work together if they were going to reverse Queen Malice's spell!

⋄Friends Forever⌐

Ellie came out of the school. The costumes were finished and she was sure they'd look brilliant in the flying competition – *if* it went ahead. Now she just had to find Jasmine and Summer and patch things up with them so they could look for the Bird Keeper together!

Madame Aviala followed Ellie into the courtyard. The pixies that the girls had seen earlier were still slumped on the grass by themselves.

"I have to do something," the headmistress said determinedly. She headed for the centre of the courtyard, calling out, "Gather round, everyone."

The pixies stood up and slowly made their way across to her, some flying on their leaves, some walking.

Just then, Jasmine and Summer flew down and landed beside Ellie. They smiled shyly at each other, but there was no time to say anything because Madame Aviala had started speaking.

"Today is the day of the flying competition," said the headmistress. "We have been working hard at our display for months. I know King Merry and everyone else in the audience will be delighted by your amazing flying skills. So I want you to set your differences aside and work together." She looked around at the pixies hopefully. "Can you do that?"

Some of the pixies looked at one another sheepishly, but most of them still looked very grumpy and refused to look at Madame Aviala as she spoke. Then one of the pixies pushed another one, who bumped into someone else, and in no time, all of the pixies were pushing and shoving each other!

As Madame Aviala ran over to try to stop the pixies fighting, Summer, Ellie and Jasmine gave each other a hug.

"I'm sorry for not listening to you," Summer said.

"Me too," said Jasmine and Ellie together.

"I'm so glad *we're* friends again, but why aren't the pixies?" asked Jasmine.

"I think it must be because only a little bit of glitter landed on us," said Summer thoughtfully. "The only way we can really help the pixies is by returning the charm to the Bird Keeper as soon as possible."

"Look!" cried Ellie. "The charm is glowing!"

"Yes!" smiled Summer, picking up Rosa and looking at the charm on her collar. "I noticed that some of the words appeared when I was helping a little pixie called Pip, but now the whole spell has appeared! I wonder why?"

"I helped two pixies practise for the competition," said Jasmine thoughtfully.

"And I helped Madame Aviala make the costumes – that was fun!" smiled Ellie.

"That must be why the whole rhyme has appeared!" cried Summer. "Even though we weren't being very good friends to each other, we were friendly in other ways."

Just as the girls were about to read out

the verse together, there was a flurry of wings and a beautiful swan appeared above the school. The girls recognised it as one of King Merry's royal swans.

The stunning white bird looked huge to the pixie-sized girls. King Merry, also shrunk to pixie-size, was sitting on the swan's back. He was wearing his best purple robe and his shiny crown. Trixi was flying beside the swan on her leaf.

Trixi helped King Merry climb off the swan's back and onto her leaf. Then she carefully steered the leaf down to the ground next to the girls. The swan flew away into the distance, its wings gleaming.

"Hello, King Merry!" the girls cried, smiling as the merry monarch climbed off the leaf. The king beamed at the girls, but then his face became grave. "Trixi called me using her magic ring and told me you've been fighting," he said anxiously. "She was worried about you!"

The girls looked down at their feet. They all felt ashamed for being mean to one another. "But we're friends again now," Summer said. "And we're going to try to make sure everyone else becomes friends again too so the competition can go ahead."

"We just need to read the verse out and call the Bird Keeper," Ellie said.

Just then the wind blew and a speck of glitter fluttered down towards King Merry. He smiled and reached out to touch it. Straightaway his face darkened! He crossed his arms and scowled at them.

"Well, what are you waiting for?" he snapped.

"Quick!" Summer cried. She hated seeing the kind king being unfriendly!

Jasmine unclipped the charm from Rosa's collar and held it out in the palm of hand. They all read out the spell:

"To bring me back, speak loud and clear,
No matter if I'm far or near.
So clap three times and jump up high,
And straight to you I'll quickly fly!"

The girls clapped their hands three times and jumped up in the air as high as they could.

After a few moments they heard a bird singing. It was the most beautiful sound, a sweet rising and falling song. The notes bubbled across the courtyard, making everybody stop and listen. Then

the Bird Keeper appeared! She was a
brilliant blue, with gorgeous lilac-and-
yellow wings. Her feathers
shimmered as she
glided above the
school.

"She seems so big!" gasped Ellie.

"Only because we're so small," Jasmine
pointed out. She held up the charm,
hoping that the Keeper would be able to
spot such a tiny thing from so high up.

The charm glinted as the sun caught it
and the beautiful bird flew down towards

it, singing more joyfully than ever. Her
tail of long curling feathers swayed
gently from side to side and gold sparkles
showered down.

"More glitter!" groaned Ellie. "We'll
have to try and keep out of its way."

Suddenly they heard loud harsh voices.
"There's the silly bird!
Catch it!"

To the girls'
horror, three
huge Storm
Sprites came
racing across the
sky, swooping to
try and catch the Bird
Keeper. The poor thing soared into the
air to escape them, but the sprites chased
her, hooting with laughter.

The bird ducked under their grabbing hands and flew down towards the school again, her wings flapping furiously and glitter showering from her tail.

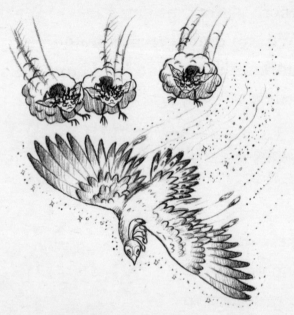

"We've got to get the bird away from here so her glitter stops making the pixies fight," said Summer, pulling Jasmine, Ellie and Trixi underneath a jutting roof so the glitter wouldn't fall on them.

"Yes, *and* we need to get rid of the Storm Sprites," said Ellie anxiously. They had to get the charm back to the Bird Keeper!

"We can do it!" cried Jasmine determinedly. "We just need to work together!"

A Pixie Plan

The girls and Trixi soared up into the air on their leaves. Ellie held on tight to the sides of her leaf, her heart hammering furiously. She was a much better flier than she had been at the start of this adventure, but it still made her quite nervous!

Ahead of her, Summer was kneeling on her leaf with one arm around Rosa.

Further off still, Jasmine and Trixi were racing along. It looked as though they were gaining on the Storm Sprites.

The sprites chased the Bird Keeper into the woods. "Get her!" they shrieked.

The bird gave loud peeping cries of alarm and her wings flapped furiously. She zigzagged first one way and then another between the tree trunks, trying to get away from the sprites, but they followed close behind.

The girls and Trixi flew on, twisting and turning between the trees. They ducked under branches and skimmed over the tops of leafy bushes.

"Keep going," Jasmine called back over her shoulder. "We've almost caught up."

Summer and Ellie leaned further forward and their leaves sped along faster than ever. Soon they were flying right alongside Jasmine and Trixi. The Storm Sprites were only a few metres ahead.

"We need to split the Storm Sprites
up," Summer panted. "But how?"

Suddenly Ellie had an idea. "Look at
all the glitter coming off the bird's tail,"
she said. "If some fell on the sprites,
they'd fight even more than they
usually do!"

"And stop chasing us!" Summer added.
"Good idea, Ellie."

"Right!" cried Jasmine. "Let's do it!"

They caught up with the Bird Keeper and the Storm Sprites in a clearing. The sprites had surrounded the bird and were trying to throw a net over her.

"You can't catch me!" cried Jasmine, whizzing past one of the sprites.

He swatted at her crossly but Jasmine was already out of reach. She positioned herself right above the frightened bird's head.

Ellie and Trixi circled round to the Bird Keeper's right. "Over here!" they called to the sprites.

Summer flew round to the bird's left. She waved her hands to attract the Storm Sprites' attention and Rosa jumped to her feet, hissing loudly.

The Storm Sprites looked round at them, trying to make up their minds who to fly at first. Suddenly they lunged at Jasmine, who quickly whizzed away.

"Missed!" she cried. She was starting to enjoy herself. She loved her pixie leaf!

The sprites whirled round then flew at Summer. She tilted her leaf to one side and flew sharply downwards to dodge their outstretched hands. She circled around and joined Jasmine and Ellie.

"Ready?" Jasmine called.

Summer and Ellie nodded.

"Now!" yelled Jasmine.

The girls and Trixi dived down towards
the ground, keeping well away from the
sparkles that were still falling from the
Bird Keeper's tail. "Over here!" shouted
Jasmine.

"No, here!" Ellie and Trixi cried.

"Here!" shouted Summer.

"Grab them!" roared the
sprites. They flew straight
down towards the girls —
right underneath the
bird's tail!

Glitter rained down on them.

The girls watched anxiously as the Storm Sprites hurtled towards them. Would the mixed-up magic work in time?

Suddenly one of the sprites stopped in midair. "Oi!" he shouted, jabbing a finger at the other sprites. "I'm going to catch that bird by myself. And I don't need any help from *you*!"

"Queen Malice picked *me* to catch the bird!" snapped another, glaring.

"You can both get lost," snarled the third. "The queen said *I* was in charge!"

"No, me!" the first sprite screeched, shaking his fists.

"I'm getting that bird, big nose!" cried the second sprite.

They began to chase each other round

and round, faster
and faster.

"Whooooa!"
one yelled as
he circled.
"I'm getting
dizzy!"

"Me too!"
another cried,
flapping down
to the ground and wobbling around in
circles. One by one the sprites crash-
landed on the forest floor.

"We did it!" Summer called delightedly
as the sprites squabbled with one another
on the forest floor.

The girls and Trixi quickly flew
back together again. "That worked
brilliantly!" said Ellie, relieved.

But the Bird Keeper was speeding away in panic. The girls raced after her. "It's okay," Summer called. "The sprites have gone. You're safe now." She didn't know whether the bird could understand her words, but perhaps she'd recognise the gentleness in Summer's voice.

The bird slowed down a little.

"Let's fly in front of her," suggested Jasmine. "Perhaps we can guide her to a branch so she can have a rest. She must be worn out."

They soared high so the glitter from the bird's tail wouldn't fall on them, then dropped down in front of her and slowed a little. Jasmine still had the charm in her hand. "Look," she said, holding it up to show the bird.

The Bird Keeper's eyes brightened.

"This way," Ellie said, steering towards a branch. Summer and Jasmine followed her lead and, to their relief, the bird flew after them. She landed on the branch, then folded her beautiful wings and looked at each of them in turn with her head on one side.

Jasmine gently stroked the bird's head and attached the charm to the collar around her neck. The girls all watched eagerly, waiting to see what would happen.

The Bird Keeper opened her golden beak and a stream of wonderful birdsong trilled out. A flash of gold spread out across her glittering feathers and the girls immediately found themselves full of happiness. They felt so lucky to be best friends with each other!

"Will you come back to the flying school with us, please?" asked Summer. "I think the pixies could do with a boost of your friendship magic, too!"

The Bird Keeper raised and lowered her head. It looked as though she was nodding. Then she spread her wings and soared up into the sky. The girls flew after her.

It only took a few minutes to reach the school. The girls were relieved to see that the pixies had stopped fighting, but they looked very disorganised and poor King Merry and Madame Aviala were running around trying to pair up all the right pixies!

Singing sweetly, the Bird Keeper flew above the courtyard. Her sparkles fell all around and all at once the pixies started smiling and laughing. Some of them linked hands and swung each other round in circles!

The bird flew back to the girls and hovered beside them with her sparkling wings spread wide. "Thank you, Bird Keeper!" they cried. They hugged her and stroked her soft, glittery feathers.

"Now you need to spread your friendship magic across the whole kingdom," said Trixi. "And we must get on with the flying competition!"

The bird cooed then flapped away, leaving a trail of golden sparkles behind her.

"I just need to speak to Madame Aviala about something," said Trixi. She winked at the girls and whizzed down to the ground to whisper in the teacher's ear.

The girls followed more slowly. The golden sparkles were still falling and each one that touched them fizzed deliciously against their skin.

They landed beside King Merry, but before they could speak to him Trixi came flying over. She looked very happy. "I've got some very exciting news!" she said to the three friends. "It's been decided that you will help to lead the competitors out for the grand parade at the start of the contest!"

"Us?" cried Jasmine. "But we're not even real pixies."

Trixi giggled. "You're pixies for today," she said. "And if it hadn't been for you the competition wouldn't be taking place at all!"

The Best Fliers in the Kingdom

A little while later, everyone was waiting for the competition to start. The pixies stood side by side in pairs on their hovering leaves, each one wearing a beautiful costume.

"I can't believe you and Madame Aviala made all these costumes," Summer said to Ellie as they flew to the front. "They're amazing!"

"Thanks," said Ellie. "It was fun... But I wish you two had been there, too."

Madame Aviala threw open the school doors. A pixie band began to play a cheerful tune and the girls flew out into the courtyard with all the pixies following them. Unicorns, brownies, elves and many other magical creatures – all shrunk to pixie-size – were watching excitedly from every side. Everyone clapped and cheered.

The girls flew right round the courtyard with the pixie competitors flying close behind. Ellie was very surprised to find that she was enjoying flying in front of everyone, despite being a long way from the ground!

The crowd craned their necks to get a better look at Rosa, sitting at the front of Summer's leaf in her acorn cup, and the little cat purred as she looked down at the amazing magical creatures below. Jasmine loved being in front of a crowd and she danced across her leaf confidently.

After two laps of the courtyard, the girls flew down to join King Merry, who was sitting in a tiny throne. Trixi was sitting beside him.

"Hello, Your Majesty," the girls
chorused.

"Hello there, dear friends!" King Merry
cried, beaming delightedly. He pointed
to three empty chairs and a pretty little
basket beside his chair. "These are for
you, girls. And one for Rosa! Come and
sit down."

As soon as the girls and Rosa were
in their seats, Madame Aviala cried,
"Pixies, let the flying competition begin!"

The first pair of pixies shot up into the
sky, their orange-and-yellow costumes
glittering brightly. They performed a
daring loop-the-loop and whizzed back
down again at top speed, like two tiny
shooting stars! Ellie covered her eyes, sure
that they were going to crash, but at the
very last minute they stopped – and with

a tap of their pixie rings, their costumes began to flash with all the colours of the rainbow. The crowd went wild!

The next pixie pair wore the butterfly costumes that Ellie had made. They spun in midair so many times the girls felt dizzy just watching them. Another duo looked like two tiny

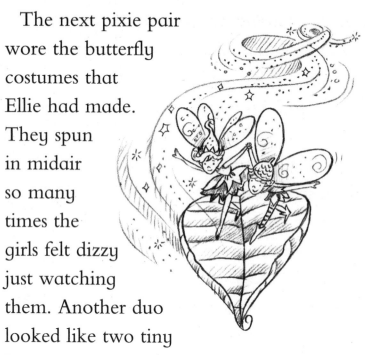

hummingbirds as they darted this way and that around the courtyard, playing beautiful music from tiny flutes as they flew.

"Aren't they amazing!" Jasmine gasped, watching two pixies perform handstands on their speeding leaves. "How is King Merry ever going to be able to choose a winner?" Suddenly she spotted Holly and Tiggs. "Those are the two pixies I helped!" she exclaimed excitedly.

The two little pixies flew along side by side, then leaped across the gap between their leaves, spinning around and throwing up their hands as they landed. They waved to Jasmine as they went past.

"They were brilliant!" cried Ellie.

The sky began to darken as the day turned to evening. Madame Aviala clapped her hands and the pixie competitors flew to the nearest roof and settled there. Only one pixie was left.

"It's Pip!" cheered Summer. She told Jasmine and Ellie how she'd found him crying in the woods. "But it looks as though he's got his confidence back now," she said, relieved.

Pip flew round in a circle, springing high into the air and turning somersaults as he went along.

Rainbow-coloured smoke spiralled out from the back of his leaf, then formed into the shape of a beautiful bird before drifting away into the sky. The audience clapped and cheered. Pip bowed quickly then flew back to be with his friends.

The band stopped playing. Everyone turned to look at King Merry, waiting for him to announce the winner.

"I wonder who he'll pick?" Ellie whispered.

The sky became darker still and thousands of twinkling stars came out. Now colourful lights shone out all around the courtyard. "Look at the glow-worms!" exclaimed Summer, waving at the little creatures, who waved their lights in the air.

At last King Merry stood up.

A murmur of excitement rippled through the crowd and the girls exchanged excited looks. All the pixies had flown so well they couldn't imagine who King Merry would pick.

"Friends," he said. "As always the standard of flying has been excellent and it's very hard to choose a winner. But, I have decided that the best fliers in the kingdom, and those entrusted with the very special job of helping to teach the other flying creatures in the Secret Kingdom pixie flying tricks are…Holly and Tiggs!"

"Brilliant!" cried Jasmine, clapping her hands delightedly.

Holly and Tiggs flew over and King Merry handed each of them a rolled up certificate. "Well done," he said, shaking

hands with them.
Madame Aviala tapped her pixie ring and whispered some magic words. At once, the two pixies were dressed in smart purple uniforms decorated with glittering gold braid.

"Those are their special uniforms," Trixi explained to the girls. "Soon the pixies will take part in a graduation ceremony to get their grown-up leaves. And then their new job will start!"

As the two pixies waved at the crowd, fireworks shot up into the dark sky and

exploded into glittering stars.

"That's it!" said Trixi as the last star faded away. "The competition is over for another year." She smiled at the girls. "Thank you so much for making sure it went ahead."

The girls smiled back. "It's been brilliant!" they said together.

"And we'll be back again soon," said Ellie. "We've still got the Lion Keeper to find!" She grinned at Jasmine and Summer and they smiled back excitedly.

"I'll send you another message as soon as I can," Trixi promised.

King Merry hurried over. "Thank you, girls," he said. "I don't know how we'd manage here without you!"

The pixies came swooping by on their leaves. "Thanks for saving our flying competition," they called. Pip stopped to give Summer and Rosa a hug, and Holly and Tiggs waved to the girls as they raced past.

As Summer picked up Rosa, Trixi gave them all a hug then tapped her magic ring. A sparkling cloud came whooshing out. It whirled around the girls, lifting them off their feet. "Goodbye, Trixi!" they called. "Goodbye, everyone!"

A moment later they found themselves back in Summer's bedroom.

"It feels so strange to be big again!" laughed Summer, putting Rosa down on the bed. Rosa meowed loudly, as if she agreed with Summer!

The DVD was still playing and the baby owls spread their wings and launched themselves into the air. "Pixie-flying beats owl-flying any day," giggled Jasmine.

"It does," agreed Ellie. "As long as you don't have to go too high."

The magical map of the Secret

Kingdom was still spread out on
Summer's bed.

"The Bird Keeper's background is
fixed now," Jasmine said, pointing
to the shield. "So she'll be travelling
around the kingdom spreading friendship
everywhere!"

As Summer folded up the map and put it back in the Magic Box, she smiled at Jasmine and Ellie. "And we know that friends are *so* important! Here *and* in the Secret Kingdom!

**In the next Secret Kingdom
adventure, Ellie, Summer and
Jasmine must find the**

Rainbow Lion

Read on for a sneak peek...

Another
Adventure Begins!

"Isn't it sunny?" said Ellie, pushing her
red, curly hair back and tilting her face
up to the blue sky.

Summer and Jasmine smiled and
nodded. The three friends were sitting
on the grass in Summer's garden. Their
parents were chatting on the patio and
Summer's two younger brothers were

playing a game with Ellie's little sister, Molly. Smoke from the barbecue drifted all around the garden.

A ladybird landed on Summer's hand. She smiled. She loved all animals, even tiny ones!

"You should make a wish," said Jasmine.

Summer shut her eyes. *I wish we could go back to the Secret Kingdom really soon*, she thought. She opened her eyes to find Ellie and Jasmine grinning at her.

"Bet I can guess what you wished for," said Jasmine.

"Could it have something to do with visiting a place with the initials S.K.?" asked Ellie.

"Of course!" Summer smiled.

The three friends shared a wonderful

secret. They looked after a beautiful magic box that magically transported them to an enchanted land called the Secret Kingdom! They'd had some incredible adventures there and met pixies, elves, mermaids and unicorns, as well jolly King Merry, the ruler of the kingdom.

The ladybird stretched its wings and flew away. "I hope my wish comes true," said Summer, watching it go. "The sooner we can go back to the Secret Kingdom the better."

The smiles fell from the others' faces as they nodded. The Secret Kingdom *really* needed their help at the moment. Once every hundred years four magic animals were released from a magical shield – a puppy, a seal, a bird and a lion cub. These were the Animal Keepers and it was their job to travel around the Secret Kingdom spreading fun, kindness, friendship and courage. When they had been around the whole kingdom they returned to the shield for another hundred years.

King Merry had invited the girls to watch the Keepers magically appear but while they had been in the Secret Kingdom, disaster had struck! Queen Malice, the king's horrible sister, had put a curse on the Animal Keepers so that as they travelled around the land their powers would be reversed – the puppy would make people miserable not happy, the seal would make people mean not kind, the bird would cause people to fight and fall out instead of being friends and the lion cub would make people cowardly instead of brave.

The girls had promised to reverse the curse. So far they had managed to find the Puppy Keeper, the Seal Keeper and the Bird Keeper and returned their magic charms to them, breaking the curse. But the Lion Keeper was still somewhere in the Secret Kingdom. They were longing to go back to try and find him!

Read
Rainbow Lion
to find out what
happens next!

Secret Kingdom

Have you read all the books in Series Four?

Meet the magical Animal Keepers of the Secret Kingdom, who spread fun, friendship, kindness and bravery throughout the land!

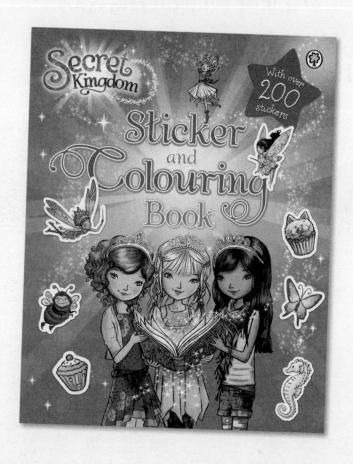

The magical world of Secret Kingdom comes to life with this gorgeous sticker and colouring book. Out now!

Secret Kingdom

Collect all the amazing
Secret Kingdom specials - with
two exciting adventures in one!

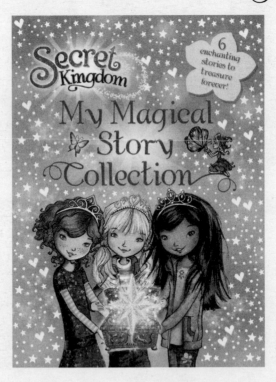

Secret Kingdom

Be in on the secret.
Collect them all!

Series 1

When Jasmine, Summer and Ellie discover
the magical land of the Secret Kingdom,
a whole world of adventure awaits!

Secret Kingdom

Series 2

Wicked Queen Malice has cast a spell to turn King Merry into a toad! Can the girls find six magic ingredients to save him?

Secret Kingdom

Swan Palace

ROSIE BANKS

Wildflower Wood

ROSIE BANKS

Snow Bear Sanctuary

ROSIE BANKS

Phoenix Festival

ROSIE BANKS

Fancy Dress Party

ROSIE BANKS

Jewel Cavern

ROSIE BANKS

Series 3

When Queen Malice releases six fairytale baddies into the Secret Kingdom, it's up to the girls to find them!

Secret Kingdom

A magical world of
friendship and fun!

Join the Secret Kingdom Club at

www.secretkingdombooks.com

and enjoy games, sneak peeks and lots more!

You'll find great activities, competitions, stories
and games, plus a special newsletter for
Secret Kingdom friends!